Cover Design by Cover Girl Design

Want a free Ebook? Join my mailing list to get my monthly newsletter!

my second CHANCE

MATILDA MARTEL

Dr. Calvin Young just turned forty. Divorced for two years, he's still picking up the pieces of his life, grieving the years he lost and waiting for his second chance to meet his first love.

Tessa Franco just turned twenty and her life revolves around avoiding intimacy. She's never had a boyfriend. Never goes on dates. But secretly pines for the only man she's ever loved—-her best friend's dad.

It's been five years since she's seen him. Five years of waiting for her second chance to win his heart.

That time has come.

ONE

CALVIN

I'VE DREADED this day for weeks. I know it's just another year. Age is nothing but a number. I'm in the best shape of my life and the greatest years are yet to come.

That's such bullshit.

Those are just words. Pathetic lies, we tell ourselves as we grieve the passing of our youth. Forty means something to me. If things were different, I might not care. But they're not, and I do.

I just wish I'd done something sooner. I wish I'd taken chances before it was too late.

With a drink in my hand, I take the quick steps onto the sand and walk into the cool ocean breeze. I left the city right after work and arrived just in time to see the sunset over the water. This is a perfect start to my week. I have seven days away from the clinic to lick twenty years of wounds and try to move on with the rest of my life.

Happier days are overdue. I might not get everything I want, but I can make the most of the time I have left.

When I was a kid, my parents loved watching the sunset every summer evening. That was their thing. Holding hands, drinking lemonade, and watching the sunset on another joyful day. Every now and again, I'd catch them dancing in the sand under the moon while my father butchered her favorite songs.

After forty years together, nothing's changed. They still live every day to the fullest and never go to bed angry. I forgot how much I wanted a marriage like theirs. In two weeks, they'll come back to this house to spend their summer by the shore. Hand in hand, they'll dance and watch the sunset every night.

I envy that kind of bliss. I'd give anything for a taste of it.

This misery has gotten old. It chafes me. It's a useless emotion, and as blessed as I've been throughout my life, I'm ashamed that I still yearn for so much more. Instead of taking in the beautiful sight before me, all I've done is stare into my empty glass and regret having left the bottle in the house. This isn't right. No more drinking. Not tonight. It's pathetic, and it hurls me into a downward spiral of regrets.

I just wish I could talk myself out of this slump. While I was married, I did it all the time. I convinced myself I wasn't utterly miserable for eighteen years when every waking moment around my ex-wife was sheer torture. The last five were only bearable because we lived separate lives and slept in separate bedrooms---a small mercy that kept me sane.

I stayed for Olivia. I didn't want my little girl to grow up in a broken home, but I should have known better. As soon as she graduated from high school, she was the one who convinced me to file for divorce.

Take the chance, Daddy. This can be your second chance to find your first love.

Two years later, those words still haunt me. Olivia was just a kid, and she saw it all along. Her parents never loved each other. That must have been hard to see and ugly to live through.

That's my biggest regret. I don't want my daughter to settle because her parents settled. I don't want her to have low expectations for love. She should reach for the stars and hold out for the one man she can't live without.

And I hope she does.

Unfortunately, I'm no closer than the day my divorce became final. I thought I'd make up for lost time. Everyone told me I needed to get out and have some fun, meet women and sow twenty years of oats. But that's not my style.

I've had four dates in two years. Four first dates that never made it past dinner. They were likable women. Attractive and successful. But I'm not wasting one more minute of my life idling in situations that bring me no joy. If it doesn't feel right, I move on.

No excuses. Never again.

When I find what I'm looking for, I'll know it.

But tonight, I'll watch the sunset alone and dream of holding my girl in my arms.

The right girl.

The one I fear doesn't exist.

TWO

TESSA

"WHEN WILL YOU BE BACK?" Olivia sits on the edge of my bed and watches me pack. After a week of asking me to postpone, she's finally come to terms with my poorly timed abandonment.

"Friday or Saturday. It depends if my Dad shows up mid-week. He swears he'll try, but that's his usual line." I fall to my knees and crawl around the bed, sure I left my sandals here somewhere---they're my favorite.

"Can you come back sooner? We're telling Daniel's parents Thursday night, and I'll need your counsel. Tessa, what if they hate me?" She hugs a pillow and follows me into the closet. Olivia's my best friend in the entire world, but she really needs to work on being less needy.

"Daniel loves you, and you love him. You're engaged with a baby on the way. No matter what his parents say, it's all about the two of you now." I squeeze her shaky hand and try to calm her nerves.

"He's eager to marry. Yesterday, he suggested City Hall, but I talked him out if it. I'd like an actual wedding. Something small but elegant with a few family members and friends. You know you're my maid of honor. I'm not asking. I'm telling." She giggles as she demands.

"I expected no less, but you need to tell your parents as soon as possible. You know they'll need time to fight, blame one another, give each other the silent treatment and then eventually come around long enough to be civil at your wedding." I tease and slip on my white cover-up sundress. It's a bit transparent, but with the flip-flops and hat, my destination is obvious. I'm hitting the beach. Six glorious days by the shore to work on my tan, read trashy novels, and sip daiquiris to my heart's content.

"Don't poke fun. My parents are not cooperative, and the stress isn't good for my skin. First, we need to tell them twice because they refuse to sit at the same table. Then Mom cancels and claims she's under the weather. *That's suspect.* And now Dad, the man who never takes a single day off, has gone on vacation for a week. Obviously, the universe is telling me to wait. I'll practice on his parents first." She reaches for a stack of perfectly folded tank tops and nervously refolds them into a mess.

"You've known for two weeks. You've been engaged for three days. I thought Daniel wanted to ask your father for your hand. What happened to that?" I pull out my toiletry kit, pull out my lip gloss, and toss it back in the bag. I promised myself I'd go make-up-free this week, but lip gloss shouldn't count. It prevents chapping.

"I know I've been procrastinating, but I swear I tried to make it happen. I invited Dad out for dinner. Yesterday was his birthday, and it's obvious he's not taking the big 4-0 very well." She whines and follows me into the kitchen. "That must be why he took this vacation, but it couldn't come at a more inconvenient time."

"Olivia! Your pregnancy is not an appropriate birthday conversation. If he feels old, telling him he's about to become a grandpa won't make him feel better." I roll my eyes and tighten the strap on my bikini top. If I can beat traffic and get this girl to shut up, maybe I can hit the sand by noon.

"No, I planned on making it special. I promised good food and ordered a cake. I made reservations at some Italian dive named Minelli's. It's god-awful, but it's his favorite. And you know what he did? He asked for a raincheck and swore he was going out of town for a week. Since when does that old man go anywhere?" She huffs with frustration.

I play it cool as my pulse jumps and my heart leaps into my throat. "You said yourself your Dad works too much. Why aren't you happy he's taking time off?"

"I'm just worried he'll be alone forever. That's why I'm taking matters into my own hands and fixing him up with one of Daniel's aunts. She was a runner-up for Miss New York back in the day. Here. Tell me if this is a good photo of him. I'm sending it to his Aunt Jenny tonight." She scrolls through her phone and hands it over.

"What do you..." I lift the phone and cast my weary eyes on the man of my dreams. I haven't seen him in years. The photo she keeps in her apartment is over a decade old and taken long before we met.

I stare briefly, mesmerized by the sight of his steel-blue eyes and the new flecks of gray dusting his temples. He's a little older, but the years have been nothing but kind. Too kind. How can any man be this beautiful? How can any boy compare to him?

They don't. That's the problem.

"It's a great photo, but I'm sure he can find someone on his own." The quiver in my voice is almost undetectable as I grab my keys and head to the foyer.

"What about you? Do you think you'll take a date? To my wedding, I mean." Her eyes grow wide with curiosity. She's an eternal busy body, and my non-existent love life is never far from her thoughts.

I have nothing to say. No updates. No realistic dreams to put into motion. Olivia won't want to hear that there's a 99% chance I'm going stag. Instead of answering with a snide comment, I avoid her gaze, pull down my hat, and slide on my sunglasses. "How do I look? Does this outfit work?"

She frowns and tilts her head. "Fantastic. You always look fantastic, but why are you wearing a hat in the car?"

"I've got my Dad's convertible. My summer is starting right now, missy!" I tap my watch and lock up my apartment.

Side by side, we race down the steps and head out into the street. As expected, she gasps at the sight of the car. "Oh, my God! You've got the Porsche! Your Dad loves this car. Why is he suddenly so generous?"

I shrug and throw my bags in the trunk. "I asked for the beamer, but he insisted and shoved the keys in my hand. His new girlfriend, Hope, is only two years older than me. I couldn't care less, but he feels so guilty he's showering me with gifts."

She gives me a side hug and a kiss on the cheek. "Take care. Don't spend all your time reading. Take a long stroll on the beach in that bikini, and I'm positive you'll come back with a man of your own." She winks and waves me off.

I laugh to myself and roll down the window. "Let me know how they take the news, but don't you dare bug me 24/7! And for your information, I'm there to relax. The last thing I want to do is fall in love."

As I drive away, I touch the St. Christopher medal on my keys and whisper a faint apology. "I didn't mean that."

THREE

CALVIN

ENOUGH FEELING SORRY FOR MYSELF. This vacation is way overdue, and as long as I'm here, I'll take full advantage of the sun, the sea, and this golden opportunity to relax. Who knows when I'll have time to come out here again? But right now, I've gotta get out of bed and start my day.

Just five more minutes. That's all I need. In five minutes, I'll drag my ass into the shower, dress, and hit the coffeehouse down the street. I can plug in for an hour, catch up on some emails and watch happier people pass on the street. Maybe some of their joy will rub off on me. You never know. Strange things happen every day, and I have a good feeling.

Something's coming. *Something good.*

I reach for the remote on my nightstand and tap a button to open the drapes.

Jesus H. Christ, that's bright.

Why did I drink so much? I swore it off, then strolled back into the house and had two more. If I hadn't stumbled on my way to the bathroom, I might have had a third. My tolerance is not what it used to be. It's been two years since I stopped medicating myself nightly, and I didn't realize I'd become such a lightweight.

I'll chalk it up to a lapse in judgment.

The bottle was in my field of vision, and my soul felt too empty not to fill it with the nearest libation. And now I suffer. I've been forty for twenty-four hours, and I already feel like shit. This isn't the way I want to start my week.

This is such bullshit---I need to stop complaining. A tiny hangover isn't a problem. I'm a doctor---I can make this better. I just need to get out of bed and start my day. Once I start my day, things will get better.

Just ten more minutes.

* * *

I won't let this bug me. Not for long, anyway. It's my vacation. It's perfectly acceptable to fall behind schedule. On the bright side, the two extra hours of sleep did wonders for my headache. But I won't lie. If I don't get a potent dose of caffeine into my system in the next ten minutes, I might die.

"What can I get you?" The server surprises me out of a daydream.

"Sorry, man. I'll have a latte." I mumble as I power up my computer and continue to take random glances out the bay window.

"What kind of milk?" His tone is unnecessarily curt. The place isn't busy enough to warrant the attitude.

"What do you have?" I know what they have. I just want to annoy him for annoying me.

He sighs. "Everything."

"What's everything?" I snap.

He clenches the pen in his hand and exhales with frustration. "Whole, 2%, Skim, Coconut, Almond and Flax"

"Fine. I'll take 2%." I answer without looking up.

"Dude, you did that on purpose. Everyone has 2%." He marches off and murmurs something about me being an angry old man. *Little shit.*

Maybe I am just an angry old man who likes to piss off teenage waiters who'd rather be on the beach trolling for tail. So be it. I'd rather be his age and have my entire life ahead of me.

If I could do things over again, I would have trolled for ass on this beach instead of worrying so much about getting into a good medical school. If I'd hooked up at least once, I wouldn't have been a horny, nineteen-year-old virgin who let his best friend fix him up with his girlfriend's friend. I certainly wouldn't have slept with a girl I hardly liked who swore she was on the pill. Of course, I'm the idiot for trusting someone I didn't know.

I can't regret having Olivia. She's the best thing in my life, and for her sake alone, I'd do it all over again. I just wish I'd left earlier.

For fuck's sake, I'm such a broken record.

"Who are you talking to?" The jackass reappears with impeccable timing.

"Myself. Obviously." I curl my lip in a defiant sneer, take my coffee and hand him my card.

"Whatever, dude." He snarks and then leaves me in peace.

Two sips and my headache slowly floats away. The pounding decreases. The pressure departs. I lean against the wall and turn my attention back to the street.

A pair of toddlers fly by, followed closely by a young father yelling for them to slow down. The sight of their fudge-smeared cherub cheeks makes me wish I'd had more children.

I'm a pediatrician. Of course, I wanted a houseful of children.

And if I'd been married to someone I love, I'm sure I would have tried. But after a few years of marriage, I had no desire to sleep with Marion. My hand was safer and brought me far more pleasure. Besides, I wanted out so badly, I couldn't handle my departure being **h**eld up by another child.

Jesus that sounds awful. I'm such a dick.

My guilty conscience is suddenly amplified when a group of teenage girls comes into sight. Screams and giggles ensue as they drool over the rail-thin teenage boy they've deemed worthy of their worship. I can't help but smile. Their braids and colorful braces pull my heartstrings and make me wish I'd invited Olivia.

We don't spend enough time together. It's not Olivia's fault---I should try harder. I know she's got a new boyfriend she wants me to meet, but I've been in such a funk I haven't made time to fit them into my schedule. I'll see her as soon as I get back.

While I answer an email, a young woman stops near the window to use it as a mirror. With the reflection of the sun beating down on the glass, she can't see the strange man staring curiously at the way she applies gloss on her pouty lips. When she rubs her lips together, my eyes helplessly run down the length of her body. She's exquisite. Lithe and petite. Curvy with long legs peeking out of a short gauzy dress. Her white bikini is easily visible through the sheer fabric, and for the first time for as long as I can remember, my mouth waters at the sight of a woman.

Stunned by her beautiful face, I'm utterly enthralled by each changing expression, every smile, and each lock of wavy brown hair blowing in the breeze. I gaze fixated and wait for her next move. I couldn't look away if I tried. She looks from side to side, removes her hot pink sunglasses, and winks. For a second, I think she sees me. My heart races as a hopeful smile creeps on my lips.

Is she winking at me?

When she peeks over her shoulder again, I know I'm wrong. She's practicing. Her bright amber eyes beam through long fluttering lashes as she pouts and poses in front of the glass. She has no earthly idea a pathetic old man is on the other side of the glass, growing hard as a rock as she rehearses her best come hither looks for whatever jerk she's meeting on the island.

No, she's not here for anyone else. She can't be.

And if she is, he can go to hell.

I'm here for a reason---she's here for a reason. *This is kismet.* Fate. I've been with one woman my whole life, and I hated every second. The trauma left me celibate for fifteen years. There are hundreds of windows on this strip, and she stopped at mine. That's not a coincidence.

Oh, please God, I've never asked for much. *Give me this girl.*

As she discreetly pushes her breasts together, I feel desperate to touch her. An unknown hunger takes control of my senses and renders me an idiot as I foolishly press my hand against the glass. It's a mistake. Her eyes grow wide with fear. She gasps, covers her mouth with a look of mortification, and rushes away. *Fuck!*

I feel shaken into action. I need to meet her. I want to say hello and hear her voice. If I don't find out who she is, I might never see her again, and I don't think I can bear it. Not now. Not after I've waited so long for this day. Without a moment to lose, I store my computer and dart out into the street.

But she's gone. My girl is gone.

In a panic, I scan east to west. My eyes search every sidewalk, every parking stall, and exit. Nothing. No one matches her description. Where could she have gone? How could she leave me?

Was she even real?

FOUR

TESSA

I'M TWENTY YEARS OLD, and I've never been kissed. I've never had a boyfriend. Except for high school dances, I've never dated. There was no need, and I had no desire. Dating is for people on the prowl. Lovers looking for their other half. I don't need to look. I know exactly where I belong, and if I spend the rest of my life looking for someone to replace him, I'd never find his equal.

Six years ago, I fell in love. Earth-shattering, mind-blowing love that shook me to my core. That first gaze crushed my heart and nearly brought me to tears. His first smile swept me away into another world where only he and I exist. There was no doubt in my heart and soul that I'd found the man I'd love until the end of time.

I know it sounds nuts. But when you're fourteen, and your heart awakens for the first time, it doesn't feel foolish. It feels natural and larger than life.

It's not like I didn't know things were complicated. My teenage brain couldn't fully comprehend the depths of my feelings, but even then, I knew I had to wait. He was older and married.

Yeah, I know. Horrible.

He was my best friend's father. *Scandalous.* And he was too good of a man to take a second glance at an adolescent girl.

But that didn't keep me from dreaming.

Every night, I dreamed our day would come. I wouldn't stay fourteen forever, and I could tell even then, his marriage wouldn't last. His misery was unmistakable. Eventually, he'd be free, and when that day came, he'd realize everything he ever wanted was right in front of him.

Of course, things didn't go according to plan.

A year into my vigil, life swooped in and destroyed my dreams. My parents, whom I always assumed were happy, went through an ugly divorce and turned my world upside down. Within weeks, they sold the house and pulled me from school. Dad moved in with his girlfriend, and Mom moved us into the suburbs of Connecticut.

But my heart stayed in New York.

On a tragic, tear-filled ride in my mother's Volvo, I vowed I'd never settle for *good enough* or *happy for now*. I'd take all or nothing at all.

I'd have Calvin Young or no one else.

So, I've waited, dreamed, and hoped for another chance. A second chance to make him mine.

That's why I'm here. That's why I'm walking on the beach towards Dr. Young's summer home in my best string bikini. He may not be there. This might be for nothing. But I need to see this through, or I'll never move on.

Calvin and I belong together.

This is inevitable. Fated. Written in the stars.

But that doesn't mean I can't give it a push.

FIVE

CALVIN

SHE'S the most beautiful girl I've ever seen. Of course, my eyes fell out of my head. Is it any wonder my heart beat so hard it felt like it repeatedly crashed into my sternum? This isn't a miracle---it isn't fate. I'm just a foolish, horny, old man who wants to believe in love. After all these years, I still want to believe the love of my life waited for me, the way I've waited for her.

But she's not real.

I couldn't find her. I spent hours walking the beach, visiting random stores, and following every possible lead from strangers who swore they saw someone resembling her only minutes before I appeared. For a brief second, I felt a tinge of hope. I caught a glimpse of a woman in a red Porsche that resembled her from a distance. She never saw the idiot flagging her down, and I'd like to assume that wasn't her. There's no way someone like that, as hot as she is, driving a Porsche, would waste her time on me.

She must be a ghost. No woman that gorgeous spends one minute in a bikini without a man tied to her hip, guarding her like a rabid watchdog. If she were mine, I couldn't bear to let her out of my sight. No fucking way would I tolerate random perverts in coffee shops getting hard while they watched my girl innocently retouch her lip gloss.

There's no use dwelling on it for now. For the second night in a row, I've come out to sit on the sand and watch the sunset alone. It isn't so bad. I'm a lucky man blessed with a good life. Maybe I was wrong about this girl. She looked young. Perhaps only a few years older than my daughter. Is that what I want? Can I handle being attached to someone almost half my age?

Fuck, yes.

If it's her, yes. I'll deal with it---I can't get her out of my mind. There was something so familiar about her. Those wide hazel eyes pierced my soul---her warm smile danced on my heart. Every inch of her haunts me like a dream I can't forget. I feel like I've known her for years, yet I've never felt anything like this before. I need to find her. I need to make this happen, or she'll become my biggest regret. And I have enough of those.

The next time I see her, I'm not holding back. I'm not dawdling like a frightened schoolboy too paralyzed to chase the girl of his dreams.

She's the one. I know it as sure as I know my own name.

And I'm not blowing my second chance.

SIX

TESSA

EARLY IN OUR FRIENDSHIP, Olivia and I discovered both our families had homes by the shore. We were thrilled. And after weeks of begging, we convinced our parents to bring us at the same time. I had the easier task. My parents were secretly planning their divorce and willing to give me whatever I wanted. Poor Olivia had to resort to faking a nervous breakdown. It was subtle enough not to send her to the looney bin, and it forced her parents to finally agree on something.

She needed a real summer vacation away from the city.

Despite her deceitful shenanigans, we had the time of our lives. For ten days, we frolicked by the shore, worked on our tans, listened to our dads argue about the best way to barbecue, and laughed about our mother's simmering hostilities.

We agreed her mom was at fault.

My mother might be overprotective and overbearing, but she's as sweet as pie. Olivia's is a holy terror. When she wasn't tearing into her husband for some perceived slight, she was nagging her daughter to death about showing off too much skin in her one-piece bathing suit and calling me a slut under her breath for wearing a bikini. Dr. Young played referee. He defended his daughter, sweetly complimented my suit but never stuck up for himself.

Even though it's been six years since I've seen their house, I'll never forget where it sits on the beach. I still see it perfectly in my mind. My heart swells every time I remember him standing in his trunks or running into the water for a swim. He was magnificent. That was the summer my lovesick heart fluttered away for good.

Olivia's pregnancy brain has been my friend. She acts like her Dad's vacation came out of left field, but she spoke about it weeks ago. She mentioned the shore but never said which one. I'm the idiot who didn't ask for details. The east coast is full of beaches. Why revisit the ugly memories he made here when he could start fresh at Martha's Vineyard or Cape May? But I have a hunch he's here.

There are no guarantees. Even if he's here, there's a slim chance he'll be outside at dusk. It's just a feeling attached to an old memory I keep close to my heart. Six years ago, I watched Olivia's father from their guest bedroom window on those warm summer nights, sitting out on the beach lost in thought. Every evening he'd gaze at the sun setting over the water, and every night, I'd fall asleep dreaming of the day I could join him.

As I tread closer to the beach near their house, my stomach tightens with unease. Six years of anxious unrequited love shatter my heart. If he's not there, if the place looks deserted, I'll have no recourse. I could spend months or years waiting for another chance that might never come.

Fearing I'll lose my mind, I pick up the pace, stumble through loose sand and jump for joy when I spot a house light. Excitement courses through my veins. I want to run proclaiming my undying love, but I temper my expectations. I need to be sensible.

After all, nothing's for certain.

Lights aren't a sure thing. It could just as easily be Olivia's mom or grandparents. And if that's who I spot through the kitchen window, my world will come crashing down around my feet. There's no need to rush my destruction. But this is a good sign. I have hope, and that's better than nothing.

As I approach the house with painfully slow steps, a tall shadow catches my eye. My skin prickles with a premonition as I spot a lone figure on the sand. It's a man. He's lying on a towel, shirtless and wet, staring up at the sky.

Oh, my God, it's him. I think it's him. *Dear God, it's really him.*

I skid to a halt. My tummy twists as my pulse quickens to a reckless pace. Calvin Young hasn't seen me in years. Not since I moved away. Not since I was fifteen years old and hardly woman enough to fill out the *Sailor Moon* style bikini I was sure would blow his mind. I just hope he thinks this one is sexy enough to see past my age. Just because I'm twenty doesn't mean he'll be able to see past who I am. Before I take another step, he looks my way and sits up.

He saw me. *Oh my God, he saw me.*

When he stands, my love-struck eyes fill with tears. Dear Lord, I've ruined weeks of plans in a matter of seconds. He can't see me this way---I'm supposed to be a mature, sexy, irresistible woman. I can't look like a big baby in a white string bikini.

Who wants that?

In a poorly considered panic, I head for the water. I need time to dry my eyes and let the breeze cool the flush off my cheeks. All I need is five minutes. I'll walk over and say hello in five minutes. Too hysterical to consider the time of day, I run straight into the chilly water and scream when the first wave douses my entire body.

"Sweet Jesus!" Water splashes my face and ruins the perfectly styled beach waves I spent an hour getting just right. Saltwater stings my eyes and momentarily blinds me. I flail about, desperate to get back to dry land but terrified I'll fall on my ass in front of him. When I swing around, a hand reaches out for me.

"Are you okay?" His warm voice is unmistakable. It's Dr. Young. *My hero.*

I fight to open one eye, grateful I talked myself out of wearing mascara. "I'm fine. It's colder than I expected."

He chuckles under his breath and leads me out onto the sand. "I can't believe you're here. You don't know how happy I am to see you."

My heart soars. He remembers me. He remembers me, and somehow, he's loved me all along.

This is a miracle.

I play it cool and fight to steady my breath. "You are?"

He nods and takes my face in his hands. "Are your eyes all right? Should we wash them out?"

Words fail me. I shake my head and feel my cheeks heat under his gaze. While he waits for my reply, my hungry eyes drink in every corded muscle of his finely tuned forty-year-old body. He's a god. Other men should be embarrassed in his presence.

I stammer in his magnificence. "I'm fine. It was just... a splash."

I'm a dork. I've got zero game, and I don't care. Take me, now. I'm ready.

He smiles and runs his finger down my nose. "We can't have anything happen to these eyes. They're the prettiest I've ever seen."

My breath hitches, and my puckered nipples grow painfully tight. This is unbelievable---he's flirting with me. Dr. Calvin Young is flirting with me.

Keep it together, Tess. Don't you dare cry again.

"I'm okay." The butterflies break free and tickle my throat.

"Will you sit with me? I was about to watch the sunset. We haven't missed it." He points at the orange-pink sky and offers his hand.

I stifle a gasp. "Sunset?"

He wants to watch the sunset with me?

I give him my trembling hand and let him lead me to his place in the sand. He's so beautiful. My heart aches to feel his lips on mine. My body yearns to feel his hands explore every inch of my skin. I've waited so long. Everyone I know has been having sex for years, and I've held out like a nun for this man alone. I'm too close now. One sexy move, and I'll explode.

When we sit, his eyes sparkle as a smile slowly forms on his chiseled face. "You don't have to be nervous. I promise I'm not crazy." That's an odd thing to say, but I'm too overjoyed to consider its meaning.

"I saw you today. I was on the other side of the glass at the coffeehouse." He kisses my hand.

Jesus Christ, kill me.

SEVEN

CALVIN

HER FACE PALES, and her shoulders slump forward. I embarrassed her. Of course, I did. Why did I say that? I didn't mean to make her feel bad. It was fucking adorable. How else would she know I'd seen her before?

"Please, don't feel bad. I'm the one who should have given you privacy. But I couldn't. I felt star-struck. I couldn't bring myself to turn away. When you ran, I chased after you. I wanted to apologize and ask you out for tonight. You don't know how badly... how much I hoped to see you again." I stare at her hands as I speak.

She's so lovely---I'm too overcome to look directly into her face. My heart feels too full. Precious blood has left my brain and traveled south, thickening my cock to obscene lengths. With any luck, these shorts are loose enough not to give away the farm. I'd hate to frighten her away.

"This might sound silly, but I had a feeling you'd be here." She bites into her plump lip as her eyes grow wide. When she tries to speak again, a lone tear streams down her flushed cheek.

This is wild. I'm not sure I truly believed in fate until now.

"You came looking for me?" My heart wants to fly out of my chest. She's an angel sent from heaven.

Her tiny nod is almost imperceptible. Her sweet voice is hardly audible. "I waited for you." She sniffles and casts her misty eyes towards the setting sun. The angle of her face. The line of her nose. Her long lashes batting with nervous tension. And those warm honey eyes that haunt me like a dream. She's so familiar.

Did I dream of her?

Where did this girl come from? This isn't love at first sight. She's too familiar. Perhaps we met in another life. For fuck's sake, I can't believe this is happening. I don't believe in any of these things, and yet suddenly, it all feels plausible.

"It's beautiful." Her tear-filled eyes drift to mine and then return to the horizon. I'm speechless. Who cries with a sunset? Her sweet ways slay my bitter soul. Her palpable innocence breaks my heart. She's a vision too beautiful to take in at once, and my sputtering heart only wants more. If she'll have me, I'll happily drown in this girl for the rest of my life.

"It is," I mumble. But I have no interest in the setting sun. I can't take my eyes off the wonder of nature sitting next to me. She's lovelier than a thousand sunsets, and I need to do or say something to make this last. To make this real.

I asked God to bring her to me, and he answered my prayers. I've never been a believer. Not totally. Maybe never. But this girl has made me one today.

If something inexplicably drew her to me. If she waited for me the way I waited for her, then this is bigger than both of us. I'm not sitting on my hands. Love is for the brave---love is for men of action. I don't care if I humiliate myself. This girl makes me feel alive. She's awakened my heart, and I won't let it fall asleep again.

Without giving much thought to smoothness or execution, I pull her into my lap, wind my arms around her narrow waist and crush my mouth to hers. She gasps, whimpers and, with a sweet smile, melts into my arms. Her lips are slick and taste like cherry. Her mouth feels fresh and naïve. She doesn't know how to kiss, and for some reason, that makes me so fucking hard I fear my rigid cock will tear a hole through these trunks.

She's divine innocence wrapped in curious anticipation. She wages no struggle. No fight or hesitation. When my tongue pushes into her mouth, a deep moan escapes her lips and sparks a lust that ignites a fiery blaze only eclipsed by the sun fading in the west. The soft hum that follows each kiss, the taste of her breath, and the warmth of her skin crumble one wall after the next. I can't defend my heart against this girl. Primal love has made me helpless, and I eagerly surrender to it.

Desperate with desire, my hands fall to the round curve of her ass and dig into her supple flesh. I lose myself in her kiss as my mind spins with avarice, and I claim this perfect ass as my own. No one else will ever touch it.

It's mine. *She's mine.*

The thought of claiming her here and now fills me with a ravenous hunger I'll never sate. Everything is happening too fast, but I don't care. I don't even know her name, and I'm ready to make love to the first and last woman I'll ever love.

She gazes lovingly into my eyes and whimpers as her arms encircle my neck and her body seeks my warmth. As I draw her closer, her skin turns to gooseflesh. Her hard nipples, visible through the thin wet fabric of her white top, grow harder as her chest grazes mine. My ragged breath falters with every touch.

I'm in awe of this beautiful girl. She feels unthinkably innocent, but her craving matches my own. With every kiss, she pushes me to take another step. Wherever my hands roam, she accepts. Whatever I give her, she takes and astounds me with her lust. Her moans grow louder as she grinds into my lap, sending me into heaven when her bikini-clad pussy rubs against the steel pipe in my shorts. Fearing I'll scare her, I stifle a growl and hold back from throwing her down on the sand.

But I won't last long.

Through kisses and moans, her soft voice emerges. My angel finally speaks. "I love you... Dr. Young... I've always loved you."

My heart sputters and crashes. *She knows me?* How does she know my name? Dr. Young? *Oh my God, was she a patient?*

I lose touch with so many after they've outgrown a pediatrician. Horrified, I pull away as shame devours me. "Dr. Young? Sweetheart, was I your doctor?"

Her expression darkens as her puffy lips quiver with sadness. "You don't know me? Why are you kissing me if you don't know me?"

My mouth falls open as I struggle to keep my pulse in check. Who the hell is she? If I ask her now, I look like an asshole. It's bigger than that. She just told me she loves me. She just told me she's always loved me. Was this girl stalking me?"

Get a grip, dickhead. No way this goddess stalked you.

While she waits, the shock on her face transforms into fury. "You really don't know? I can't believe you're like this. Do you just kiss random girls you approach on the beach? What kind of man are you?"

The insinuation sparks my anger. "Of course not." I run a frustrated hand through my hair. "I saw you earlier today. You're the most beautiful girl I've ever seen, and I searched all day for you. When you said you hoped you'd find me here, I thought you'd seen me through the glass, or maybe this was fate. I don't know. I'm so sorry. This feels like fate." I pull her back into my lap and bring my forehead to hers. I need to feel her close. I need her warmth to banish the cold ache that consumes me daily. In a few brief minutes, the pain of not having her in my arms threatened to swallow me whole.

"You weren't my patient, were you?" I whisper, unsure what I would do if she said yes. "Please tell me you're over eighteen."

She chuckles sweetly and kisses my forehead. "I'm twenty. The same age as Olivia."

Olivia? How does she know Olivia?

"You know my..." My heart stops as memories flood into my lovesick brain. Teresa Franco. *Little Teresa Franco.* She was a pretty little thing. Olivia adored her and cried for weeks when she moved away. She was here. Years ago, she was here, at this house, for one of the worst weeks of my life.

How could I forget her?

Oh, my God!

Reality hits. I just had my hands all over little Teresa Franco's luscious ass, and I loved every fucking minute of it. I could have kneaded her flawless mounds for hours.

I jump to my feet and inadvertently toss her onto the sand. "Teresa?"

She quirks an eyebrow and dusts herself off. "Only my Nonna calls me Teresa. Everyone calls me Tessa."

"Tessa, I'm so sorry. I didn't realize it was you." I choke on every word as the lump in my throat grows larger by the second. All I want to do is sweep her into my arms and carry her into the house, but she's my daughter's friend. I can't be with my daughter's friend. It's obscene. Lecherous. Scandalous.

And chastising myself doesn't help one bit. I'm only getting harder.

She lifts a hand to silence me. "Don't mention it. This was my mistake." With tears in her eyes, she pivots in the sand and walks away. I want to chase after her. Every step she takes shatters my heart and rips my soul in two, but my feet remain glued to the sand. I can't be that guy. I can't be the sleazy man who sleeps with his daughter's friend.

I'm a pediatrician, for fuck's sake.

Jesus Christ, this is a nightmare. Of course, she feels familiar. I'm such an idiot. Unfortunately, my whiskey-soaked brain couldn't pinpoint exactly why she felt like an old friend. And not my friend. *Olivia's friend!* This was never fated or miraculous. This is nothing but an old pervert hitting on his daughter's best friend.

And why the fuck am I still hard?

EIGHT

TESSA

OH, my God! I can't see where I'm going. It's too dark, and I was too heartbroken to count the houses after I fled in disgrace. Even the clouds conspire against me.

The trickle of moonlight seeping through the overcast skies is hardly enough to help me distinguish one house from the next. This is such a disaster. I need to get home. I need to change out of this damn bikini and order a pizza. I've starved myself for the past two weeks on the chance I'd see Calvin Young.

And for what? He's nothing but a gigolo, and I'm nothing but a fool.

Olivia has him pegged all wrong. She thinks he's a lonely, sad shell of a man who hasn't dated in two years.

What a joke!

She doesn't know he lurks around beaches, luring unsuspecting girls to watch the sunset just to cop a few feels and pinch their behinds. How could I be so gullible? I thought we were soul mates who'd fall into each other's arms and promise our life and love forever. I thought I'd spent the next few weeks arguing with Olivia about how much I love her father and insist she calls me Mommy just to make her laugh.

I'm a dummy. A big, blind dummy who can't find her way home in the dark.

Clutching my broken heart, crying my eyes out, I stumble through the sand in search of my father's house. It's coming up. It must be coming up soon. Why didn't I think to leave the deck light on?

"Tessa!" A voice in the wind makes me pick up my heels. I think it's him. If it's not him, it's a man, and I have no use for men. I'll never trust them ever again.

"Tessa!" He calls again, but a break in the clouds illuminates my dad's pool and makes me veer to the right. I run at full speed. I don't care if I look insane. I don't care if I fall and need to crawl the last few steps. If I can make it inside, I can lock the door and freeze him out.

"Please, stop. I'm sorry." He's gaining. His bellow is just over my shoulder, but I bound up the deck and fly past the pool.

"Leave me alone. Go home!" I crouch to the floor and scramble as I search for my key under the mat.

"Tessa, I'm so sorry. Please forgive me. I didn't mean to hurt your feelings." He grabs my key, but I snatch it out of his hands. Every word stabs my heart.

He's sorry? Those precious moments meant the world to me, but he sees them as a lapse in judgment. A horrendous mistake he'll want to forget. I don't need to make him feel better when I feel lower than dirt.

"Shut up! Shut up! Shut up! You're making things worse! I don't want to hear your apologies. You're only here because of Olivia. I won't tell her anything---it's too humiliating. Please, leave." I aim for the keyhole, but he blocks my path with his body.

"Please, listen. I don't want you to think badly of me. I don't do this. You're the first woman I've kissed since my wife, and it's no secret how much I hated her. If you weren't who you are, wild horses couldn't keep me away from you, but I just can't. I'm so sorry." Affection and remorse swim in his beautiful blue eyes, but I can't listen. I'm seconds from bursting into a sniveling, blubbering fit the likes no one has seen since my cat, Nicoletta, passed away eight years ago.

Nothing he utters makes me feel better. Every word shatters me into a million pieces and scatters me into the sand. I'll never recover. I'll never be whole again. But I played my cards, took a chance, and now I can move on knowing I fought for love.

No regrets, Tess. That's what matters.

"Thank you, Dr. Young. You must think you're a kind man for coming here to let me down gently. But I don't care. I don't care about you, and I don't care about tonight. You may leave with your conscience intact. I wouldn't dream of sharing this horrible experience with anyone. Goodnight." I push my way past him, but again, he hampers my efforts.

"You said you loved me. You said you waited for me. What did that mean? Why did you say that?" His wounded expression shocks me.

What the hell does this man want? Does he *want* me to pine over him?

There's been enough of that, *thank you very much*. I know I'll never get over him. I know I'll carry this forever. Why does *he* want *me* to suffer his loss?

Move along, jackass. I'm not here to stroke your ego.

"You must have heard wrong. I never said those things. Go home." I slam the door so hard the tiny brass anchor hanging over the frame falls on his head.

Good. I hope it left a mark.

NINE

CALVIN

I SHOULD LEAVE. Reason dictates a swift departure, and I like to think I'm a logical person. Nothing good will come from staying.

Frankly, I don't trust my strength.

I've never felt anything like what I felt last night, and my resolve grows weaker by the minute. If I stay, I might run into her. And if I run into her, I may say or do something foolish.

She deserves better. She deserves a man her own age just starting out in life. I'm too old. I've got too much baggage for such a sweet, innocent... girl.

Innocent. The word lingers in my mind. Thoughts swirl and dive into a dark place. She said she's always loved me. She said she waited for me. What exactly does that mean?

I'm a sick man.

Her possible virginity does nothing to frighten me away. It just makes things worse. My need grows stronger. My thoughts grow filthier. If she saved herself for me, who am I to turn her away? Her innocence belongs to me. Every inch of that girl could belong to me.

You don't turn away a gift like that. It's thankless.

Why am I so hard on myself? I've been with one woman. I've been celibate for over a decade. For fuck's sake, I'm practically a virgin myself.

No, I can't do this. Thinking about it makes me want to give in, and I can't. How could I possibly show my face at Christmas or Thanksgiving dinner with my daughter's best friend on my arm? She's young---she'll want children, and I'll want them with her. How would it look if beautiful, innocent Tessa, half my age, is pregnant with my baby? Everyone will know I've spent weeks plowing that fertile field night and day like the lecherous fiend I've become just to ensure the entire island of Manhattan knows that gorgeous girl is marked for my seedy desires.

Goddamn, that wasn't supposed to get me hard.

I swear, I've tried to be a good man. I stayed up half the night practicing speeches and words of consolation that seemed patronizing at best. None of them feel right. It's not what I want to say. It's not what I need to do. I've waited forever to feel half of what I'm feeling right now, and if I throw it away, I'll never get a second chance.

I won't deserve it.

Maybe this is a test. After all, I've bitched and moaned for years. I railed into the wind and cursed my lot in life, longing for a day I never truly believed would come. Not everyone gets to fall in love. I know that. I made my peace with that long ago, always secretly hoping I was wrong. And maybe I am. Perhaps this is my chance. I think it is. Tessa could be my second chance to fall in love.

Fuck, yes. This is my chance.

I get to fall in love. Someone beautiful and wondrous loves me. She says she's always loved me.

Damn it, she took that part back.

That had to be a lie. She wanted to put me in my place, and I can't blame her. She had every right to treat me with indifference. I minimized her feelings. She gave me an incredible gift, and I refused it, citing nothing more than my daughter's discomfort as a reason to break her heart.

Tessa wasn't my patient. She's not underage. I knew her for a short while years ago, and we were never close. This is hardly taboo. It's weird for Olivia, but I think she'd want me to be happy.

We'll talk. I'll apologize, and we'll talk about last night. She caught me off guard. It's not a bad thing that I couldn't remember her---she was fifteen years old the last time I saw her. I had no business giving her a second glance. *And I didn't.*

Grown-up Tessa Franco is an incomparable woman. A woman like her comes around once in a lifetime. What kind of fool would I be to walk away?

Things were said in the heat of passion, but nothing is irreparable. We both said things we didn't mean. Maybe. I know I did. But what if she didn't? What if I was just a schoolgirl crush she's finally gotten out of her system?

There's no sense in driving myself crazy. I need to see Tessa. Really see her. Snooping into her bedroom window at 5:ooam doesn't count. I don't know what possessed me to go at that hour. But I couldn't sleep, and I needed to be near her.

Thankfully, she didn't see me. After forty-five minutes of watching her sleep, I came home, cried into my oatmeal, talked myself off the ledge, swore her off, then spent the rest of the morning jerking off to memories from last night.

Two days ago, I didn't think I could be more pathetic.

I was wrong.

TEN

TESSA

"SO, HE WAS JUST STANDING THERE?" Alex stares in amazement as he sips his cappuccino. He wasn't thrilled leaving his hot boyfriend in Sag Harbor, but the peeping Tom story made him fly out of bed and join me for breakfast. "To what end?"

I shrug. "I don't know. You're a man. What do men do?"

"Do you think he was beating the salami?" He smirks.

"Salami? *Heavens.*" A delicious image appears in my mind.

"And why didn't you call the cops?" He points his fork in my direction.

"Why would I call the cops? The man was staring at me while I slept. This is progress. There's no freaking way you would have called the cops if Professor Gonzalez was peeping through your window." I wave a half-eaten croissant at him.

He gasps, then chuckles. "Number one, Oliver Gonzalez isn't gay. But if he magically converted and peeped through my bedroom window, I wouldn't just lie there like a pot roast and not give him the best goddamn show of his life. Why the hell didn't you walk around naked? You could have stripped under the covers and strutted casually to the restroom. Maybe even throw in a few stretches. Where's your creativity? Don't you have any pride in your work? You've been planning this seduction for weeks." He butters a piece of bread while he chides.

I shrink in my seat. "I don't want to give it all away for free. He's done nothing to deserve a peep show. It's supposed to be special. You know what they say about the cow and the milk."

He narrows his eyes. "Why buy the cow when you can get the milk for free? Is that the ridiculous phrase you're referring to?"

I nod and reach for my water.

"You're such a virgin. So, you give away a little free milk. Big deal. You know what else comes from cows?"

My eyes grow wide. "What?"

"Cheese. Butter. Yogurt. Gelato. Cream, Tess. Lots and lots of cream. You give him a little taste of milk, and you bet your sweet tits he'll be back for the cream." He smiles and stabs his fork into my quiche.

"Cream? You're sick." I snicker under my breath and shove a piece of bread in my mouth.

He laughs. "You don't fool me. I read your diary. There's some messed-up shit in there. That poor man is being pursued by the nastiest virgin in New York."

I kick him under the table. "That diary was ancient, and I still haven't forgiven you."

"But you don't deny your perversions, huh?" He steals another piece of quiche. "Now, hurry. Let's get out on the beach and piss this guy off."

CALVIN

I'VE TRACKED HER DOWN. It wasn't hard. She's swimming in her pool, sunning her gorgeous body, and having the time of her life with some obnoxious beefcake who insists on reapplying oil to her delicate shoulders every fifteen minutes.

What kind of suntan lotion washes away that quickly? If she needs a better brand, I'll buy it and apply it myself. That oaf is taking advantage of her obvious desire to combat sun damage. How unchivalrous. How opportunistic. One more application, and I'm coming out from behind this bush and crushing him to a pulp.

What the hell am I doing back here?

Late this morning, I showed up with flowers. I don't believe Tessa was home. That's a lie. I know she wasn't home because I peeked through every damn window to make sure the house was empty. These are not my finest moments. But I'm at my wit's end. I need to see her and say I was wrong. I'll shout it. I'll drop to my knees and beg her forgiveness.

Last night, meeting her again, holding her in my arms, and tasting her kiss meant everything. I've waited so long to meet the love of my life. How could I have known all I had to do was wait for her to grow up?

This is ridiculous. I'm a grown man. A respected physician. I'm lurking in the bushes like a crazed stalker, ogling her while I rub my cock through my shorts. It's beneath me, someone might see, and it's not doing any good, anyway.

I want the real thing---and I had it. I had Tessa in my arms, ready and eager to be taken. She wanted me as much as I wanted her. Instead of hiding and creeping, I could've been tilling that virgin soil and planting my seed all fucking morning.

And what's gotten into me? I've never farmed a day in my life.

This is too much. I can't take a chance and wait for this dickhead to apply one more layer of lotion. She needs to know I haven't stopped thinking about her. She needs to know we can make this happen if she gives me another chance. I don't know where this handsy jackass came from, but he's irrelevant. She said she loves me. I saw the tears in her eyes when she confessed her feelings. She meant it. God knows I don't deserve her love, but that doesn't mean I can't earn it.

With hope in my heart and every ounce of courage I can gather, I march up to her deck stairs, ignore the asshole in the pool and walk towards her lounger. She drops her book and lowers her sunglasses.

"Dr. Young." Her mouth falls open as her wide honey eyes lock on mine.

"Calvin. Please call me Calvin." My eyes run over every inch of her twenty-year-old, glistening, oil-soaked body and helplessly land on the full, round breasts peeking out from her flimsy bikini top. My heart stops. My brain freezes. I can't look away. They're breathtaking. Indescribably beautiful. When her stiff nipples join the party, my voice flees, and I stare dumbfounded at the last pair I'll ever hold.

This girl is mine, and I'm not leaving this island without her. She needs to say yes---*yes, to dinner, yes, to spending the night, and yes, to spending the rest of her life with me.*

If she turns me down, I'll only come back tomorrow and ask again.

"Calvin? What are you doing here?" She sits up and uses her book to shield her overflowing cleavage.

I shake my head to clear my mind, relieved it breaks the spell long enough to state my intentions. "May we speak?"

She nods but stops. "You said everything you had to say last night. You don't want to get involved with your daughter's friend."

I hang my head, and my eyes drift toward her supple thighs. The same thighs she wantonly wrapped around my waist in the throes of passion. The same ones I want to wrap around my face until I hear her scream my name. I want to feel them again. I want them around me always.

"Tessa, I didn't mean it. I'm sorry. I panicked and tried to do the rational thing, but nothing feels rational when I look at you. I wanted you before I knew who you were, and that hasn't changed. Judging by some things I've done the last two days, it will only get worse. I'll deal with Olivia. She always says she wants me to find someone who makes me happy. Last night was the happiest I've felt since I was a kid. I want more. I want you... if you'll let me make it up to you."

She lifts her book to cover her face, and I whimper at the sight of her mouthwatering breasts.

Through sobs and sniffles, she replies, "You don't know how long I've loved you. If you're not sure you can deal with this, it's better we..."

I take her tiny hand in mine and slide in closer. "I am sure. Let me take you to dinner tonight. I haven't seen you in years. I want to hear everything I've missed. Because from this day forward, I won't miss anything else."

As we stare into each other's eyes, lost in this sacred moment, a voice beckons from behind. "Hey Tesscakes, can I go back to Sag Harbor now?"

TWELVE

TESSA

"SO, tell me. What sort of fifteen-year-old girl develops a crush on a man twenty years her senior?" His sultry voice croons as his steel-blue eyes impale my heart.

Dinner was lovely, romantic, and the food was delicious. We dined alfresco near the shore and watched the sunset from our table. We shared our plates and talked about the last five years of our life. His divorce. My studies, likes, and dislikes. We've giggled over silly anecdotes and struggled to get through the awkwardness of what's to come when his daughter and my parents find out about us. And now, as we sip our coffee, his latent curiosity of my long unre-quited love has finally bubbled to the surface.

I nibble on my cookie and turn to look at the rolling waves. What sort of girl, indeed? I never thought of it as unusual, but most girls that age fall for the high school quarterback or the goth guy who never smiles. Not me. I couldn't be bothered with boys. I wanted a man. More specifically, I wanted this man. I was desperate for this beautiful man and thought day and night about what I would say when this day finally arrived.

How can I convey the depth of my love and lust without sounding like a foolish little girl?

Something comes over me. A thought morphs into an emotion that spreads like wildfire throughout my limbs and into my core. With a sudden surge of confidence, my eyes meet Calvin's, and I answer his question the only way I know how. "If I had to guess, I'd say she was a naughty girl."

His eyes flare. The air simmers. He wasn't expecting that, but with a smile, he sets my heart at ease.

"A naughty one?" His eyebrows arch mischievously. "Explain yourself, young lady."

I nod and take a sip. "Doesn't that sound naughty to you? A young girl falling in love with her best friend's father and saving herself exclusively for him. Never kissing other boys. Never petting in the back of cars. Saving every special first for a man twenty years her senior. That sounds pretty naughty to me." When his gaze falls to my chest, my taut nipples grow painfully tighter. My panties dampen, and my thighs quiver with need.

He licks his lips and leans closer. "Was I your first kiss?"

I flutter my lashes. "You were. I'm sure you could tell."

He swallows hard. "I had a hunch. But you're beautiful..."

My lips part in surprise. "I didn't say no one wanted to kiss me. You don't believe you're the first who's tried, do you?"

He takes my hand. "Who tried to kiss my girl? Give me names, and I'll take care of them personally.

I stifle a grin and take a slow sip before I answer. "You don't strike me as the jealous type."

"I'm not. At least, I wasn't. Just because I was married doesn't mean I've ever truly been in love. What I'm feeling now, what I feel for you, I've never felt before. Jealousy is an unfamiliar emotion. The thought of anyone else sniffing around you makes me see red." His jaw clenches, and his gaze smolders, consuming me into a fiery pit of hot, raunchy lust.

My heart pounds. My stomach knots. I feel flushed and so incredibly horny, I think I might burst. All these years, I refused to sample the many goods tossed my way. I held out for Calvin Young. This gorgeous, sexy man sitting across the table, undressing me with his eyes. But the time is now. If he doesn't move quickly, the place might be here.

I need action. I need cock. *Haven't I waited long enough?*

"You've never been in love before?" My voice shakes. That seems highly unlikely, but I need to move this discussion to its foregone conclusion, or better yet, his place.

He shakes his head. "No, not 'til now. I never believed I would fall in love, but now I know I was just waiting for you." He kisses my hand, and the tingle buzzing in my belly crackles into an electric charge. Our eyes clasp in a wordless exchange as we sit in black silence, lost in each other's gaze. One more word of love, and I won't be responsible for my shameless actions. I don't want to be a virgin anymore---the pressure's too great, and I've loved him too long. I'm ready.

For heaven's sake, take me now!

A waiter appears. "Can I get you anything else?"

"No!" We shout in unison.

Calvin clears his throat and hands him his credit card. "Thank you for everything. Please hurry."

THIRTEEN

CALVIN

SOMETIMES THERE'S bliss in torment. This love affair just launched. We should wait, but I've waited twenty years to fall in love. Twenty years to make love to a woman I worship with every breath. I never expected someone as glorious as Tessa. I didn't think I'd feel so much so fast. Logic screams I should be cautious. After my horrible divorce, I should take my time and not run head-first into love. But my heart has overruled my brain, and my mind never put up much of a fight, anyway.

This is fate. This is a miracle, and I won't question it with doubts that serve no purpose.

My father always said, *when you know, you know*. I thought that was bullshit. Something lucky men who fall ass-first into love say to validate their good fortune. But now, I'm one of those lucky bastards, and they were right all along.

When you know, you know. I don't need weeks, months, or years to figure out if I can spend the rest of my life with Tess. I know without a doubt, I can't live my life without her. She's my home. The one I always wanted.

And she's not getting away. Not now. Not ever.

FOURTEEN

TESSA

HIS PLACE IS CLOSER. The moon is out. Stars have aligned, and love is in the air. I'm not walking seven more houses to unwrap the only gift I've ever wanted. Without a word, I lead him up the steps to his door.

He *knows* what's coming. I *know* what's coming.

This might be the beginning, but in my heart of hearts, this has been six years in the making.

It's showtime, and I've got the lead role.

With one hand wrapped around my waist, holding me close, he scrambles to unlock his door. We fumble into the darkness, his lips on mine, my arms on him. There's nothing between us now. No doubts or misunderstandings. We're just two people falling in love and stepping into the rest of their lives. My wildest dream and fondest wish are coming true.

In the dark, my senses sharpen to his taste, his scent, and the warmth of his breath. I tremble with suspense as his hands caress my face, smoothing every angle with thick fingers I want to pull into my mouth. I want to feel and taste every inch of his heavenly body. Whatever he wants is his. Whatever he needs, he can take.

Heart and soul, I belong to him. I always have, and now I know for sure, I always will. When our mouths meet again, the world falls away, and my lovesick heart finds peace.

Lost in another world, I stare, confused as he pulls away. His gaze and sweet smile greet me with a kiss to my forehead and a breathy sigh. "Are you certain? We can wait..."

I've had enough delays. I lunge forward and seal my lips to his, longing for more and desperate for this cruel teasing to end. Fearing I need to take matters into my own hands. I back away and begin unbuttoning my blouse.

"Where's your bedroom?" I raise an eyebrow and pull off my top as I march to the back of the house.

"Straight ahead." He catches up in time to tug me to him and pull down my skirt.

"Eager little thing, aren't you?" His husky voice prickles my skin.

I nod and kick off my sandals. "Will you let me undress you?"

His eyes widen. "Is that what you want?"

I don't wait. With trembling hands, I pull Calvin's shirt over his head and softly gasp at the sight of his chiseled chest and rippled abdomen. His powerful arms rest at his sides and his stern gaze falls on me. Reality sets in. We're minutes from making love, and nothing will ever be the same again.

"Let me help you." He lifts me into his arms and crushes me to his chest. My legs hug his waist. My arms seek his embrace. With a move I don't detect, he unlatches my bra and throws it on the floor.

Claiming my mouth, he devours my lips, filling my mouth with his tongue and coaxing one kiss after another until we melt and fall into the bed. I could kiss him forever.

"I love you, Tess. I don't deserve you, but I promise you won't regret me." His mumbled whisper makes my heart clamor in my chest.

"Calvin, I love you. I've always loved you." I whimper as his lips trail wet kisses down my shoulder and across my chest before he swallows a tight nipple in desperate need of his undivided attention.

There are no words. His kisses don't stop. Switching from one breast to the other, he suckles hard, teases my flesh, and sends currents of sexual adrenaline tingling into my thighs.

I can't breathe---I can't speak. My body shivers with uncontrolled desire. My legs tremble as sparks of lusty bliss engulf me and shoot me into outer space. His lips, his tongue, the warmth of his mouth, the sight of him suckling my breasts summons cries followed by wails I have no strength to contain. Ecstasy finds me fast, and I willingly drown in a sea of pleasure.

Calvin stares, bemused. "Did you just come?"

I don't answer. He knows I did, and I'm too embarrassed to admit I've orgasmed with such little provocation. I can't help it. He said he loved me. I'd lost hope long ago I'd ever hear those words---but he did.

Calvin Young loves me.

He pulls away and stands by the bed. With a flick of his wrist, he unzips his jeans and lets them fall to the floor. My eyes fall to the erection tenting his boxers. *Dear lord.* I bite my lip to stifle a gasp. Adrenaline triggers my flight instinct, but I will it away. I'm up for the challenge. This is the man I love, and servicing that enormous cock is the price I must pay.

It's not a difficult choice.

"Why are you smiling? Is my girl thinking naughty thoughts?" Calvin leans forward, grabs the hem of my panties, and drags them off my legs. "Baby, you're soaked."

I pout and feign shyness. "That's your fault. I warned you I was naughty."

When I try to close my thighs, he reaches out to hold them open. "Will you do something for me? Something naughty?"

I nod. "I'll do anything for you."

I freeze when his massive hand cups my sex. "Will you make yourself come? Will you let me watch?"

I gasp. "Dr. Young!"

We exchange a wicked smile.

"That's even better, baby." He runs his finger down my wet slit and strokes my clit. "Call me Dr. Young while you do it."

FIFTEEN

CALVIN

SHE CLAMPS HER THIGHS SHUT, then lets them fall open. "But can you stand it?" Her fingertips graze her breasts as they drift down her tight abdomen and settle on top of my hand.

"Will you be able to stop yourself from joining in, Dr. Young?"

I shake my head. "I make no promises, my love." I slide my hand from beneath hers and use her fingers to take tiny strokes across her swollen clit.

"Do you think you can make yourself come while I watch?" I swallow hard and watch the bloom on her cheeks trickle down her heaving chest.

She nods and uses her finger to spread her wet lips. "Drop your boxers and show me what's waiting for me at the end."

"Whatever you want, angel." As I tear them off, my stiff shaft slaps my abdomen and makes her flinch. Her eyes widen with curiosity. Her legs spread another inch. It's all here for the taking, and I'm dying for a taste. But I haven't had sex in fifteen years. Once I taste her and sink into her virgin flesh, I don't expect to last long. If I can make her come multiple times before we begin, I won't need to hang my head in shame for ruining her first experience.

"Is this what you want?" She shudders as her fingers make lazy circles around her sweetest spot.

My taste buds sting as my mouth waters. "That's exactly what I want. Rub harder, Tess. Pretend your fingers are my tongue because that's coming next."

She arches her back as her hips grind into her hand. "I'm so close, Dr. Young. I'm going to come right here in your office. Won't I get in trouble?" My pulse spikes. She's so good. *Such an artist.* This is a thousand times better than the nastiest pornography I've ever seen. This beautiful girl, my beautiful girl, is giving me exactly what I want without hesitation. There's no way I deserve this. Not a chance.

I can only assume I rescued orphans in a past life.

I lean closer, inspecting her work while her tiny fingers work their magic. She's unbelievable. I'm so fucking in love, I may have to marry her before the end of the week. "Come on, Tess. Stick your fingers inside. Show me where you want me."

"I want you right here, Dr. Young. I want you so deep and so hard. I've waited so long to feel you inside me." Her fingers glide into her slick pussy, and she teeters on the edge of another climax. The sound and sight make me lose my mind. I can't wait for my cue. My cock has siphoned so much blood from my brain, I fear I'll faint. And I can't let all of this go to waste.

Without warning, I take her by the waist and slide her back, crawling between her legs in lusty preparation. But her fingers never stop. She's too close to cede control. While her body writhes, lost in another world, I fight the urge to join her. I won't ruin it. Her dewy skin, rising flush, and dazed expression tell me she's close enough to taste it. With her free hand, she caresses her breast, tugs a nipple, and torments me with a vision that will linger for weeks. My girl's the best kind of sadist.

A cry breaks through the eerie silence. I crawl forward to watch her face as lusty whimpers escape her gorgeous lips, and she tumbles freely into ecstasy. It's so incredible, I almost come in my hand.

"Dr. Young!" Her hips fly off the bed, and her hands grasp the sheets for purchase. I'm stunned by the heavenly sight of the woman I love writhing with pleasure, and I want to give her more. I need to claim every inch and make her scream to her maker for mercy. I can't wait another second. I wipe the drool from my mouth and dive in.

The taste of her virgin pussy brings a smile to my face, and I float into a heaven I never believed real. Her heavy scent fills my senses, and my pulse rises with every lick. My heart beats wildly as images of our future flood my mind. Everything between us is sacred. Basking in her warmth makes twenty years of wretched loneliness disappear in seconds. It was all worth it. I'll never take a second of my life with Tessa for granted.

I spread her thighs and lick a slow trail down the line of her slick pussy with painfully slow strokes. Her hard clit greets my tongue, and with each pass, her cries grow louder as pleasure boils and tension builds. When I close my mouth around that sweet spot, lashing it mercilessly as I suckle, she grabs my hair, and a feral scream echoes off the walls.

"Dr. Young..." Her soft voice trails off as her tiny limbs thrash, and I draw out one more climax with my fingers.

"No more, Dr. Young. We're making love, and I want to hear my name." My lovesick eyes stare in quiet wonder at the girl who flew in like a dream and changed my world overnight.

"Are you ready for me?" I drive my tongue deep inside her, feasting on her honey and savoring the taste of my first and only love.

After everything that's transpired, she ducks her head and nods demurely. My heart flutters with love. She's so warm and ripe, like the prettiest peach ready to be picked.

"Please, no more waiting... Calvin." Her breathy sigh fuels my lust.

"No more waiting."

SIXTEEN

TESSA

MY HEART CAN'T TAKE MUCH MORE. Every minute in Calvin's arms, every shared kiss, and look of love push me to the brink of tears. He's owned my heart since I was too young to know what love meant, and yet it never faded.

The harder I tried to stop loving him, the more he came to me in dreams and urged me to wait for my chance. I didn't think I could love him more. And yet, in two days, I've fallen into a never-ending abyss from which I'll never recover. This is only the beginning, and I'm forever lost to this beautiful man.

With bated breath, I watch him. That chiseled body, those sparkling blue eyes, those masculine hands are coming for me. My unsteady gaze drifts down his cut abs and lands on the massive cock jutting out between his thighs. My jaw drops. It's perfection. Nasty, glorious perfection.

I won't lie. It's frightening, but I'm sure my needs eclipse my fear.

When he drapes his body over me, the feel of his weight makes me lose my breath. His scent, his warmth, the intensity of this moment makes my eyes bristle with tears. When his eyes find mine, he smiles, rubs his thick cock against my clit, and dips it into my wetness. I shamelessly spread my legs wider. I need him like I need air, and nothing's stopping this from happening now.

"I love you, Teresa Franco. You're my first, last, and only love." His velvet voice makes my heart sing with joy, and his words melt my heart forever.

I bring him closer and encase him in my limbs. "I love you, Calvin Young. Only you. Always, you."

I take a deep breath and prepare for this exquisite pain I've waited so long to feel. I'm ready.

Dear God, I'm so ready.

When he hesitates to stare lovingly into my eyes, my patience falters. Hugging him tightly, I bring my hips up and feel him sink in halfway. The pain startles me, but my senses awaken to the delicious torture of being claimed by the man I love.

"Tess!" He pulls out, terrified he's wounded me.

"Calvin! Stop teasing me. Don't be gentle. Don't make me beg."

His gaze smolders. "Such a naughty girl. So eager to be plucked?"

I nod. "Lucky you."

He pulls my hands over my head and crushes his mouth to mine. I quickly lose myself in his lips, his taste, and the feel of his stiff head nudging my clit with every move. With our lips sealed, I brace myself, and he thrusts forward, shredding my innocence and filling me completely. Our hands lock, and our breaths mingle as he stretches me open with every plunge. Awash with pleasure, I hold him tighter, reveling in the feel of his invasion until my sleek channel molds to him, surrendering without a fight.

"Calvin..." I whimper for more, and he happily gives me every-thing. Friction distracts me as I learn to take him. The more he gives, the wetter I become, and the easier he splits me in two. My body welcomes every thrust. My heart thunders with love. I want all of him, every day for the rest of my life.

"Tessa, you're so tight, baby. I won't last." He groans as he drops my hands and brings my knees forward. "Where do you want my cum? I've got so much to give you. Tell me where you want it." When he pulls out and thrusts back in, he builds a tension that sends me into another world. My hips tremble, bucking wildly as the friction grows stronger. Every kiss brings me closer to bliss.

I gasp, hold my knees and let him sink even deeper. "Inside me, Calvin. This time, come inside me. Tomorrow come on my breasts, in my mouth, on my ass —mark everything as yours."

"You're unbelievable. And I'll hold you to that."

His corded arms flex as he holds his weight off, barreling in and gliding out, while my pussy flutters around his shaft. I cry out, whimpering against his shoulder, clawing his back, thrashing against his hot skin while wave after wave of savage lust tears through me, and I dive into ecstasy.

"Calvin, I'm coming!" I grasp his sweaty chest and arch my back as this gorgeous man, *my man*, breaks me in and claims me as his woman.

"Not yet, baby. You'll make me come. You feel too good to stop now." He brings my hands over my head and, with two more powerful thrusts, sends me over the edge.

"Calvin!" My breath hitches as sweet friction carries me to the apex and toss me over the mountain. Lost in oblivion, my cries fade as he crushes his chest to mine, covers my mouth with a smoldering kiss, and accepts my unqualified surrender.

"Are you sure you want my cum inside you? You know what that could mean." He whispers against my lips, and I melt into a puddle of hormones.

I nod. "Yes...please. I know what it means."

"I'll always give you whatever you want... I love..." His words drop as his body tightens. His arms pull me closer until there's nothing between us. While he whispers inaudible words of love, his growl vibrates against my chest, and his pulsing cock fills me with rope after rope of hot seed.

This is the beginning of everything, and I'll never get enough.

SEVENTEEN

CALVIN

I WAKE up sore and spent with an angel curled in my arms. Last night was the most incredible night of my life. I'm madly in love, and I can't wait to drag this girl down the aisle. She's loving, sweeter than any woman I've ever met, and so fucking insatiable. My life is made.

If it wasn't for my fifteen-year dry spell, she might have given me a run for my money, but my ravenous lust for her gorgeous body gave her no peace. Even now, I have a hunch she's feigning sleep to escape the stiff boner poking her back.

Desperate for another round, I brush the hair off her shoulder and nuzzle my face into her neck. "Sweetheart? Are you awake?"

She fakes a snore.

"You're not escaping so easily. You promised to ride me, and you fell asleep." I roll her over and make her straddle my hips.

She holds her breasts in her hands, leaving most of her milky flesh exposed. I pull her hands away and cup them with my own.

"I'm exhausted, baby." She whines. "You kept me up halfway through the night."

"Sweetheart, I am so hard. Feel me." I bring her hand behind her hips and make her grip my rock-hard erection.

Her face lights up. "This might be too hard. You could hurt yourself."

"Make it go down. Come on, baby. Do it for me." Before she can say no, I lift her by the waist and slowly bring her down on my shaft.

Her tight pussy takes me in, and I feel every inch of her gushing walls stretching open just for me. When my cock touches her cervix, and my balls feel the curve of her ass, I bring her forward on my chest. I take her puffy lips, still swollen from hours of kissing, and seal this sacred union with one fiery kiss after another. She's the most beautiful woman in the world, and she's mine. *All mine.*

"Calvin! You're too much." She complains through moans.

"You can handle it, Tessa. You handled it all night long." While her perfect tits bounce in my face, she grinds ruthlessly, setting a ferocious pace and wild rhythm. We kiss, lick, and nibble on every piece of skin we can reach. Nothing remains untouched. Nothing comes between us. As I watch her writhe and roll her hips with lovestruck eyes, my heart races with love for this crazy girl. I'll never get my fill.

Holding her hips, I thrust back. I can't thrust deep enough. Primal lust clouds my mind as my visceral need to claim her pushes me towards my climax. I need to know she's mine. I want to see her belly grow with the fruit of this all-consuming desire, and I want anyone who looks at her to know she belongs to me forever.

She's not on the pill. She confessed last night after our third round, but I assured her I suspected it all along. This is what I want. Us and our family. I've never felt anything like this. This is madness, but everything about our love makes me feel like I could climb the highest mountain.

I pull her close and thrust with a savage pace. She tries to keep up, grinding and bouncing on my cock, racing me to the finish line while her screams grow louder and her words of praise stumble into incoherent gibberish.

"Calvin!" Her descent comes fast. Flailing and rocking, she loses her breath, stiffens in silence, wails into the ether, then falls freely into a euphoric oblivion that makes her eyes roll back in her head.

I'll love this woman until I die. *Longer if I can.*

"Dad!" My daughter, Olivia, barges into our room. Tessa gasps, freezes, and falls forward, shielding her breasts on my chest.

"Tessa! Oh my God! Dad!" Olivia's mouth drops open as I roll Tessa off and cover her with a blanket. When her boyfriend walks in and sneaks a peek at Tessa's naked ass, I lose my shit.

"Both of you, out! Wait for me in the kitchen. Now!" I bark at the pair of party crashers and wrap a sheet around my waist. "Now!"

"Dad! What are you doing with Tess! You should be ashamed of yourself!" Olivia stomps out, looking strangely heavier than the last time I saw her.

"I should go." Tessa peeks from under the blanket. "I can't believe she's here. I haven't checked my messages since yesterday afternoon. This is not the way I wanted her to find out."

"Don't you dare leave---she might as well get used to us now. This won't go away. She can accept us, or she can bitch and moan for the next twenty years." I kiss her tear-stained cheek.

"What happens in twenty years?" She raises an eyebrow.

"Well, she'll be forty. Your forties mellow you out." I laugh and watch her honey eyes go wide.

"What is it?"

"I can't believe I had sex with a forty-year-old man. How scandalous." She smiles through tears and rests her head in my lap.

I tug her hair, bring her face to mine and kiss her sassy mouth. "You're half my age, and you could barely keep up."

She gasps. "I kept up just fine. I'm new to this, and I was working with some hefty equipment. I think the State of New York requires a special license to operate that kind of equip... for crying out loud. Olivia is waiting." She shakes her head and giggles.

I take her beautiful face in my hands and gaze into her warm eyes. "I'm telling her we're getting married. Are you okay with that?"

Her eyes narrow. "I didn't hear a proposal, Dr. Young."

I chuckle. "Sweetheart, you were screaming so loud last night, you would have missed a bomb going off over Long Island Sound. But I asked, and I'll ask again with a ring once we're back in the city. I want her to know we're not fooling around. This is our life. Me and you from now on."

Her eyes well with tears. "You make it impossible to be sassy with you, mister. Of course, it's okay. But I have a feeling she'll play this to her advantage. I won't betray her confidence, but she's here for a reason. She has news. News you won't be thrilled to hear. Remember that when her rant goes over the top."

I kiss her hand. "I love being a team. I love you, Teresa Franco. I love that sassy mouth. And you better believe I have plans for it once everyone leaves."

She points to the door. "Just go. I want to speak to her after you. If she's willing."

EIGHTEEN

TESSA

"GETTING MARRIED? You're marrying my father? Tessa! Have you lost your mind? He's twice your age. He's my Dad!" Olivia's arms flail about in anger as we take a slow walk on the beach to discuss this strange turn of events. I let her vent. She has a right to be shocked. She has every right to consider this a betrayal of our friendship.

But I hope in time, she'll warm up to it.

To make matters worse, the jig is up. As soon as Calvin confessed our plans to marry, Daniel jumped the gun and ruined her upper hand by announcing their engagement. News of her pregnancy slipped out minutes later. Olivia hates losing her leverage. He'll get an earful on the way back to Manhattan.

"May I speak?" I interrupt her tantrum.

She frowns as she nods. "What do you have to say for yourself?"

"I love him, Olivia. I adore him. I fell in love with him the very first time you introduced me. Why do you think I never wanted to be with anyone else? I saved myself for him. For six years, I've hoped that one day we'd meet and fall in love." I sigh and look away---I don't want to cry in front of her. Pity shouldn't motivate her forgiveness.

"Did he know?" She snaps sarcastically.

"Of course not. Your Dad didn't even recognize me when we met here. Things just happened. I know it's fast, and it looks crazy, but we realized we're the other half that's been missing all these years. Now that we've found it, we don't want to live without it." Saying it out loud makes it real. I know he and I are in this together, but I don't want to lose my best friend. Straining to hold back a flood of tears, I walk away to give her some space.

"Hey! Where are you going?" She hollers as she chases after me.

I wave her away. "I gotta go home. I'll come back."

She gains. "Are you crying? Tessa Franco, are you crying?"

"No!" I wipe my tears and run at full speed.

"You're crying! Come back here!" She runs after me.

I'm no match for her speed. Olivia was a track star. Cursing my name into the wind, she hurdles a little boy's sandcastle, flies through the air, and tackles me to the ground.

"For Pete's sake, Olivia! You're pregnant! Think of the baby." I land face down and scramble to get away.

"He'll get older, Tess. Will you still want him when he's fifty? I don't want him hurt again. If he loves you as much as he says he does, he won't live through your loss." She helps me up.

"Yes, of course. We want children---we want to spend our lives together. This isn't a crush. I'm madly in love with him. I'll love him when he's sixty and seventy and eighty." I dust myself off and walk towards my place.

"Ew! Eighty! And he wants babies? How can you do this to me? My baby will be older than his aunt or uncle!" She pushes me forward, and I stumble in the sand.

"Oh, shut up. You've been bitching for months about your poor, lonely Dad. Now, you don't have to worry about him anymore. I'll take care of him." I wag my eyebrows. "I'll take excellent care of him."

"Cut that out! Am I supposed to be okay with my best friend being my stepmom? This feels so weird and gross." She whines.

"And here I was hoping you'd call me Mommy." I clench my fists with excitement.

I finally got to use that line.

"You've been practicing that line. Haven't you?" She smirks and walks with me the rest of the way.

I nod. "Longer than I can remember. And I am so sorry. I know this feels creepy, but I really love him. Big love. Forever love. Plus, think on the bright side."

"What bright side?"

"I've got a date for your wedding!" I jump in the air and kiss her cheek.

She exhales with exasperation. "And what about Daniel's Aunt Jenny? I text her photos of my Dad for the past three days. What the hell do I tell her now?"

I laugh out loud. "That skank is not my problem. Your Dad is mine. M-I-N-E. Mine. And if your Mom sniffs around him again, I will take her down with a swift roundhouse kick to the head. Just like this." I demonstrate my moves and almost lose my balance.

She giggles. "I'd pay money to see that."

NINETEEN

TESSA

THREE WEEKS LATER

MY FATHER HAS NEWS. He called it Big News with a capital B and capital N. If my hunch is correct, I'm getting a new step-mom. The timing's perfect. The dreaded day has come, and I'm not making the same mistake as Olivia. Leverage is leverage, and this is the ideal time to share my joyous tidings.

Three weeks ago, he introduced me to a twenty-two-year-old girl named Hope with long legs, big boobs, and a flawless blonde pony-tail she wore high on her perfect head. She looked like a living Barbie doll, but Dad swore she was an old soul who made him happier than he's ever been.

Although there were brief moments of confusion and horror, I said nothing negative. I'm not a hypocrite. She seemed nice, and if Daddy thinks she's the one, who am I to judge?

Fearing my rejection, he lent me his prized Porsche and funneled a sizable amount of cash into my dwindling checking account. He said he wanted me to have fun. According to him, I'm too much like my mother and don't enjoy life nearly as much as I should.

I have a feeling he's ten minutes from a healthy dose of stunning remorse on that front.

"Are you sure this is the right moment, baby? Restaurants never work. People assume the other party won't make a scene, and it always blows up in their face." Calvin takes my hand as I lead him into *Monsieur Le Blanc's*. It's Daddy's favorite place in Upper Manhattan and conveniently located two blocks from Calvin's brownstone. I moved in two weeks ago, but I'm not comfortable calling it mine yet.

Not until next week.

"I've procrastinated long enough. We get married in eight days." I scan the room from left to right and search for any signs of my father. He's notoriously late, but considering today's topic, his nerves might light a fire under his ass and force him to arrive on time.

Calvin kisses my hand. "I begged you to let me speak to him earlier. This feels wrong, angel. You don't steal a man's daughter and tell him over French cuisine. You talk to him man to man over brandy or whiskey."

I scoff and bring my narrowed gaze to his. "Steal me? Brandy? Whiskey? I'm not a fat little cow to be bought and sold for three lambs and six chickens. I belong to no man, sir."

I take a step into the dining room, but Calvin winds his arm around my waist and stops me dead in my tracks. "I beg to differ, my love. You better believe you belong to me."

His deep growl is nothing more than a whisper, but the warm vibration against my cool skin prickles my skin and makes me stifle a giggle. "You know what I mean." I pat his hand and look over my shoulder. His piercing blue eyes smolder with a latent fury that will probably involve corporal punishment of the nastiest kind.

"Your rebellious spirit better be nerves, young lady." A smirk replaces his frown, and heat blooms between my thighs. He's incorrigible, and my exploding libido only encourages him. In three weeks, this man has turned me into his love slave.

"Not here, Cal. I think I see Daddy. Don't get ahead of yourself. Let me do the talking, or I swear to God, I'll cut you off and go live with my mother until the wedding." I release his hand and march ahead.

"No, you won't." He chuckles. Dr. Know-it-All thinks he's God's gift to my panties. We'll see about that.

"Yes, I will," I whisper and wave at my father.

"No, you won't." He pulls out my chair and offers my confused father his hand.

Goddamn it.

"Sweetheart?" Daddy refrains from shaking Calvin's hand. Maybe he can't see it. His eyes look as though they're about to fly out of their sockets.

"We should sit." Calvin and I reach for Hope's hand, and she politely shakes one after the other before helping my petrified father into his chair. An awkward unease hangs over the table while we exchange insincere pleasantries.

"Thanks for meeting us," Hope speaks for her tongue-tied date.

"Thank you for inviting us." I swallow the lump in my throat and try to get a read on my father's stony expression.

"I don't believe I invited him. I invited you." My Dad's harsh response is unexpected. And pretty ballsy for a man dating *Malibu Barbie.*

A nervous laugh escapes before my eyes flash fire. "I told you I was bringing a date. Calvin is my date, Daddy."

Calvin groans, unhappy with his classification.

"Excuse me, that's not what I meant to say. I mean, Calvin's my… lover." Bubbles of nervous laughter burst out at once. Hope follows suit and spits white wine on the table.

"Teresa Franco! Have you lost your ever-loving mind!" Daddy slams his hand on the table and nearly lunges for Calvin's throat.

I hold my hand out. "Stop that! I'm twenty years old, not sixteen. Why did you bring me here? You're getting married, right?"

Hope nods, but Daddy remains silent.

"Right?" I stand firm.

"Well, you've ruined my *Big News.*" He straightens his lapels and takes a sip of wine, utterly oblivious to the hypocrisy of his anger.

Calvin's finally had enough and addresses Hope. "How did your father take it?"

She shrinks in her seat. "We haven't told him yet."

"I see." Calvin and I chant in unison.

"Little girl…" Daddy thinks he's going to bring me down a notch, but I quickly put an end to his ambitions.

"No, sir. You ruined my formative years by leaving my mother for one of your girlfriends. I forgave you because you're my Dad, and I wanted both my parents to be happy. Now you tell me you're marrying a woman two years older than me and twenty-five years younger than you. You should be ashamed of yourself. We could be sisters!"

I don't care. Not in the slightest. But my outrage is as good as his.

He interrupts me. "Sweetheart, it's not like that. We're in love."

I shush him. "We're in love too. Madly in love. Calvin and I are closer in age than the two of you. We're getting married. Mom knows, and she's already given us her blessing." I flash my ring and snuggle into Calvin's embrace.

He tries to speak, but Hope's hyper-clapping catches him off guard. "Oh, my goodness. Congratulations! You need to tell us where you're registered."

Maybe she is an old soul.

"We're sorry to tell you this way. I would have come to you sooner, but Tessa wanted to wait. I love your daughter with all my heart. With everything I am. I wasn't looking to fall in love with someone half my age, but when you've waited all your life to feel this way, you know it's a gift. Tessa's a gift. I'll never take something so precious for granted. We're marrying next week, and we'd like you to come." Calvin squeezes my hand and then promptly hands me his handkerchief.

"What did I tell you about getting sentimental?" I whisper through faint sniffles.

"I know. I'm sorry." He kisses my forehead.

"Give me some time to get used..." Dad tries to be stern, but Hope chimes in and puts an end to his mischief.

"Of course, we'll be there. It's a happy occasion." She pokes Dad's ribs and gives him a kiss on the cheek. "Your daughter's getting married. We're getting married. Stop being such a pain in the ass and order champagne!"

TWENTY

EPILOGUE- A WEEK LATER
CALVIN

"ARE YOU HAPPY?" I hold my wife's warm body close to mine and gaze into the most beautiful eyes I've ever seen. She's breathtaking. And she's mine. All fucking mine.

We recited vows. Exchanged rings. Ate cake. Drank too much wine. And when all was said and done, ended the evening as husband and wife. It was the perfect night.

I'm a happily married man madly in love with his wife. I've become the man I always envied.

But now it gets even better.

The guests have gone. The moon has risen, and we're alone at last.

"I married the most handsome man in the world." Tessa rests her head on my chest. "I couldn't be happier."

My heart swells with love. "I'm sorry we didn't have a big wedding. You deserved a big church affair with an obnoxious dress and twenty bridesmaids fawning over you." I twirl her under my arm and guide her down the stairs onto the sand.

She skips a few steps ahead and spins with glee. "But this is exactly what I wanted. I wanted the sound of the ocean. I wanted the sand between my toes. And I wanted to end the evening where we started." She drops to her knees and unfolds a towel in the sand.

"I want to make love on our spot. The place we first kissed. The place we fell in love." She drops a strap on the flimsy slip she calls a dress and curls her finger. "Come here, baby."

My eyes burn into hers. Blood rushes south of the equator, and my cock thickens with breakneck speed. When she bites her lip and smiles, I lose my head and tackle her onto the towel.

"Calvin!" She giggles as I reach under her dress and rip off her baby blue wedding panties.

"That's my something blue. Don't lose them." She searches the sand for remnants of lace, but it's too late. Only shreds remain.

"I'll buy you more." My lips silence hers in a fiery kiss that pulls her attention back to our moment. The moment she wants to recreate. The night we almost made love in the sand.

"Calvin, I love you." Her soft lips press to mine, and our breaths mingle through every torturous kiss. I drop the second strap on her dress and let her breasts peek through the gauzy material. I don't want to undress her completely, but I want to feel her tight nipples graze my sunburned skin.

"Tess, you're so fucking beautiful. It's been a month, my love. One month and now you're my wife." My voice breaks with emotion as my hands slide up her thighs and dig into the supple skin of her voluptuous ass.

"Calvin, I need you." Her tiny hands work my belt, then undo the zipper.

"No, I need you!" I lift her into my lap and wet my cock on her gushing slit.

"Now. Please." She wraps her arms around my neck and seals her lips to mine. "Give it to me. I want the whole damn thing."

"I'll always give you what you want, baby." I ease in slowly, then gasp when her tight walls strangle my cock without mercy. Her body shudders, her eyelids droop, and her lips part in a silent scream that looks like unbridled bliss. All I want to do is dive in with her.

My hands grip her thighs and spread them wider, angling her into a perfect position to take my cock deeper. My heart beats wildly. My breath labors as I set a ruthless pace. With every thrust, my lips find hers, and she begs me to give her more. The harder I thrust, the faster she rides. Nothing slows her down.

She wasn't kidding. *She wants it all.*

"Calvin... keep going..." Her soft whimpers break me. Adrenaline pushes me to the limit. Love and ecstasy consume my senses. My lips fall on hers and with every kiss, I feast unreservedly on my beautiful wife. I'll never get enough.

"I love you, Tess." I hold her gaze and study her flawless face. Time seems to stop. Every thrust moves slower and feels twice as strong. She grinds into my lap, undulating as her body welcomes me over and over.

"I love you. I've always loved you." She grinds and pulls me and in out of her slick passage. The tension builds fast. With each pass, my cock swells on the verge of eruption. She's so wet. So tight. When her flesh contracts around my cock and her frail body ignites in waves of violent ecstasy, I unravel with her.

"Tess..." I thrust deeper, harder, and faster. My kiss drowns out her screams, and my body tenses as streams of hot cum erupt inside her. But I keep going. It slides down her thighs and onto my lap, but I keep going. We want a family. We want our life to start now, and what better place than where it all began.

"Calvin..." With a breathy sigh, she falls onto the towel, and I cover her shivering body with mine.

"You said you were a naughty girl, my love. You weren't kidding." I curl her into my arms, and my heart bursts with love.

She giggles and tucks my spent cock back into my pants. "I warned you. Now you're stuck with me."

"Yes, I am. I'm the luckiest man alive."

TWENTY-ONE

EPILOGUE- TWO YEARS LATER
CALVIN

AS THE SUN SETS, I watch my Tessa walk towards the water carrying our son high on her chest. Protective as always, she won't let the cool water splash his feet but gets him close enough to throw shells into the waves. We're here with Olivia's family and our parents for the Fourth of July and Caden's birthday. He turns one on the 3rd, and with any luck, another baby will join him before he turns two.

But no matter what comes, whether we have one baby or ten, my heart is full. The emptiness is gone. Tessa blew into my world like the ocean breeze and gave me the life I've always wanted. She's miraculous. The incarnation of love. As long as I live, I'll work hard to prove I'm worthy of such a gift.

Not everyone gets to fall in love---*but I did.* I've fallen blissfully in love, and each day, I fall in love all over again.

From my place on the deck, I watch her frolic through the surf in the same white bikini she wore two years ago. She loves to wear it when we're here alone, re-enacting that night with a much naughtier ending. It's a shame we can't do it tonight.

But there are other things.

With the sun dipping lower, I take the steps onto the sand and call out to my wife and son. Tessa waves Caden's hand, curling his tiny fingers in her thumb as she trudges towards me. Before she can speak, I take them both into my arms.

"What are you doing?" She laughs with delight and lets me take Caden from her tired embrace.

"Dance with me." I wrap my arms around her waist and, with Caden between us, lead her into a waltz.

"Have you been drinking?" She giggles as she follows my lead, traipsing through the sand under the rising moon while I hum her favorite song.

I shake my head and smile. "Nope. I'm drunk on love. My parents did this all the time when I was a kid. They'd dance under the moon for no other reason than to celebrate the end of a glorious day. But every day with you is glorious. Every day is better than the one before."

She covers her mouth and fights the start of tears. "I almost didn't come that week. I almost didn't walk the beach to find you. What would have happened if I didn't?" She breathes a heavy sigh and rests her head on my chest.

"We would have met again at Olivia's wedding. I would have found you. We're not an accident of fate. I was always meant to love you." I gaze into her amber eyes, the ones that first stole my heart at the coffeehouse window, and bring my mouth to her quivering lips. As always, my beautiful girl melts in my arms.

When we pull apart, she whispers. "When I was sixteen, I made a promise. I'd have you or no one else. Coming here was my second chance to make you love me. And you did. You made my dreams come true."

"Don't stop dreaming, angel. This is still the beginning."

Thanks for Reading!

FOLLOW ME

Matilda is a Texas girl in love with a Philly boy who loves to write dirty books about two people who trip into love and fumble their way into a Filthy, Funny, Happily Ever After.

I live in Austin, with my husband, two crazy Chihuahuas and an even crazier cat. And I spend most of my day writing dirty romance books about older men who fall in love with younger women and make fools of themselves trying to win their hearts.

If I had to describe my type of romance, I'd say I write steamy, humorous contemporary romances dipped in sugar.

If you love Dark Romance, you've come to the wrong place. I don't like dark heroes.

I like my hero to be successful, sweet, suave, sophisticated and kind--- and then I want him to lose all his composure and game when he meets the heroine. I want him to turn into a bumbling idiot when he spots the girl of his dreams and revert to a teenage boy in a man's body trying to win her.

I like my heroines to be witty, intelligent, and unshakeable---who could do just as well without a man--until the hero convinces her otherwise.

I write A LOT OF AGE GAP--because I LOVE AGE GAP ROMANCE. I've got no other excuse for it.

No matter what kind of story it is, my ladies are ADORED, and my endings are always Happily EVER AFTER, not HFN.

Please head to my website to learn what's in the final stages and will be coming out soon!

My Heart's Desire

Lana Howard is a modern-day matchmaker with the happiest clientele in Manhattan. She promises to learn your heart's desire and she delivers.

Liam Fitzgerald wants nothing to do with a matchmaker. He's fine, the way he is. But before his beloved mother passed away, she fought tooth and nail to book his secret appointment fearing her first born son would never marry.

One look at Lana and he's sold. He knows what he wants. He wants her. But Lana has a system. She doesn't give people what they want- she gives them what they need.

According to her blueprint, they're not compatible. She has a code. Flings don't turn into true love. There must be something that'll stick--- or maybe this matchmaker's been afraid of love all along.

Can Liam convince Lana they'd make the perfect match?

This is a steamy instalove, matchmaker, fling to true love, older man younger woman romance with a guaranteed happily ever after. Happy Reading!

Takeover

George Hagan is an industry titan. He's played the game for over a decade and gobbled up competitors left and right.

Winifred "Winnie" Barnes is a shiny new rock star developer, and her thriving start-up is running circles around Hagan's corporation.

He wants to take over her company, but she plans to go down fighting.

Tensions rise. Tempers flare. And a strange attractions simmers. George soon forgets about Winnie's company and sets his sights on winning Winnie instead.

George wants the whole package and the more he chases, the more Winnie runs in this sticky, sweaty game of cat and mouse full of laughs, baby-making sieges and a guaranteed happily ever after.

Lucifer

LOVE REDEEMS

Lucifer walks among us. Leading an army of fallen angels, he still takes orders from above. Good cannot exist without evil. Man's faith must always be tested. It is his job to tempt you. It is your job to walk away.

He hates his role. He hates our world. He hates Man.

But he still seeks redemption.

The Archangel of Light wants to go home and for the first time in 7000 years he has a shot.

Unfortunately, his long-awaited forgiveness will only come if he gives up the only person he's ever loved.

Livia De Lucio comes from the Light. Descended from angels she's caught Lucifer's eye.

Her pure heart intrigues him.

Her beauty enthralls him.

Her love will redeem him.

This is a paranormal, slow burn romance with a devilishly handsome fallen angel, no horns or tail, a woman descended from Nephilim who works for the Vatican, a little bit of violence, archangels, fallen angels, a couple of cardinals, a nun, and a love story about the Angel of Light who finds true redemption in love.

Love Revealed

Yuri Ivanov leads the most powerful Bratva in Brooklyn and commands attention wherever he goes. He's used to making demands and watching people fall in line. Until he meets a young, idealistic assistant district attorney and falls head over heels, obsessively in love.

Rosalind Dunne wants nothing to do with gangsters. Her father was a hitman for the Irish mob and she knows all about the destruction they leave in their wake. Since he died, she's dedicated herself to going after the mob, righting wrongs and saving the world case by case.

Her work is her passion. She has no time for gorgeous, lovesick mobsters with wild green eyes who woo her like she's never been wooed before.

So what if his sexual prowess knocks her socks off. Surely, men this hot are a dime a dozen. Right?

This is the third installment in the Brooklyn Bad Boys Series. Each book is a standalone but they always make more sense when they're read in order.

This book includes, minimal references to an attempted kidnapping and violence. Sexy times. A few peeks at past couples. A swoon-worthy alpha who falls madly in love for his headstrong heroine. No cheating. And a very Happily Ever After.

Love Unleashed

Leo Moretti always gets whatever he wants. No questions. He's his father's son and the blood in his veins is enough to make people fear the consequences of disappointing him.

Except Alia de Alba.

Alia's bold, beautiful and audacious. Her refusal has him on edge. When she turns down his marriage proposal, he incurs her wrath by playing the hero and manipulating her into marriage.

She wants to make him pay, but his hotness makes it hard. He swears they're soul mates but fears she loves someone else.

Can Leo win her heart?

Of course, he can. Leo Moretti always gets whatever he wants

This slow burn turned torrid affair includes one Sassy Latina, one hot Sicilan mafioso, love, lust, sexy times, various Pavarotti references, kidnappings, mobsters, two people who fall madly in love and a guaranteed happily ever after.

Love Interrupted

Igor Ivanov is a mob lawyer who's fallen head over heels in love with a senator's daughter.

Charlotte Wentworth is a Park Avenue princess who's in way over her head.

Madly in love, they defy their families and elope.

But after three blissful days, everything implodes, favors are called in and the two desperate lovers are torn apart.

Powerless and clueless, they part ways and spend four miserable years apart.

When a heartbroken Charlotte is finally allowed to come home, she wants answers. When Igor learns the truth, he wants things made right and more than anything he wants his Charlotte back.

He let her go once, he won't make that mistake again.

Can he convince Charlotte he's the same man she fell in love with? Or will four year of secrets, lies and threats tear them apart again?

This is a steamy second chance romance with two soul mates who fight the odds and crawl their way back home. Grab a cookie, sit into your favorite chair and meet Charlotte and Igor. As always, no cheating and a guaranteed happily ever after!

Filthy Love

Filthy Rich

Play Right

Shut Up & Kiss Me

Maestro

Lucky Man

Clever Girl

Magic Man

Agreeably Arranged

There She Goes

The Perfect Nanny

A Hostile Takeover

The Good Girl

The Pastor

The Trophy Wife

My Dad's Best Friend

My Fake Husband

Queen of Two Hearts

Closing Daddy's Deal

The Girl Next Door

And many more!

For updates on new releases click here and a free ebook, click here:
www.matildamartel.com

www.ingramcontent.com/pod-product-compliance
Lightning Source LLC
Chambersburg PA
CBHW031434130726
47989CB00003B/1141